MANSA MUSA

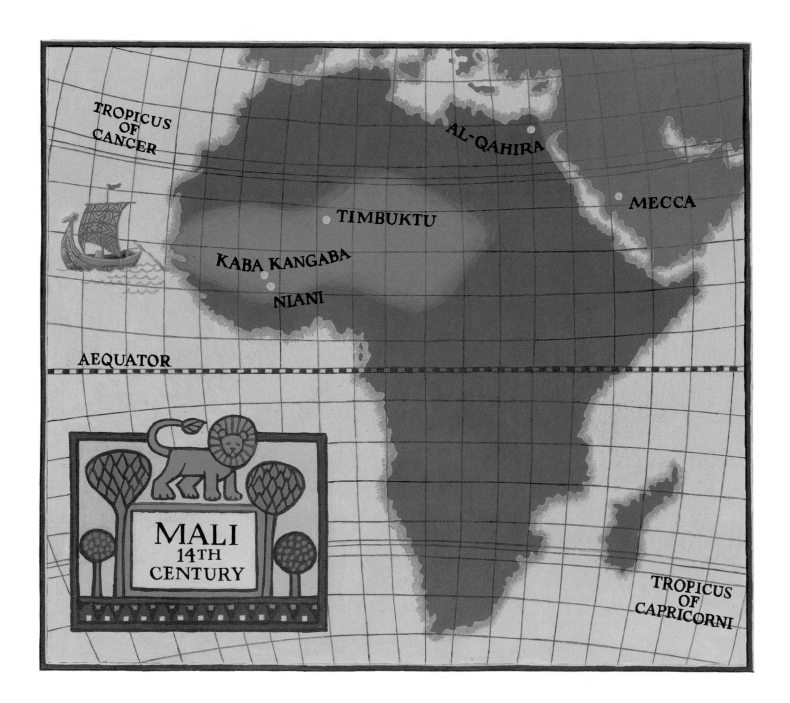

MANSA MUSA

The Lion of Mali

By KHEPHRA BURNS

Illustrated by LEO & DIANE DILLON

GULLIVER BOOKS
HARCOURT, INC.
San Diego   New York   London

www.harcourt.com

Gulliver Books is a trademark of Harcourt, Inc., registered in the
United States of America and/or other jurisdictions.

Library of Congress Cataloging-in-Publication Data
Burns, Khephra.
Mansa Musa: the lion of Mali/Khephra Burns: illustrated by Leo & Diane Dillon.
p. cm.
"Gulliver Books."
Summary: A fictional account of the nomadic wanderings of the boy who grew up
to become Mali's great fourteenth-century leader, Mansa Musa.
1. Mali (Empire)—Juvenile fiction. [1. Mali (Empire)—Fiction. 2. Musa, Sultan
of Mali, fl. 1324—Fiction.] I. Dillon, Leo, ill. II. Dillon, Diane, ill. III. Title.
PZ7.B9287Man 2001
[Fic]—dc21   97-50559
ISBN 0-15-200375-4

First edition
H G F E D C B A

Printed in Singapore

The illustrations in this book were done in gouache on Bristol Board.
The text type was set in Aries Display.
Color separations by Bright Arts Ltd., Hong Kong
Printed and bound by Tien Wah Press, Singapore
This book was printed on totally chlorine-free Nymolla Matte Art paper.
Production supervision by Sandra Grebenar and Pascha Gerlinger
Designed by Leo and Diane Dillon and Ivan Holmes

To my granddaughter,
Amina Suzanne King.
May your life be filled with
dreams and adventure—K. B.

To Anne Davies for her vision,
and to Tarik, Antar, and
Tasherit Johnson—L. & D. D.

I n the years after the death of the great King Sundiata, the glory that had once surrounded the kingdom of Mali began to fade. But the empire still extended many weeks' travel from the capital, Niani, to where the shea butter trees no longer grew. And the Malinke were still a proud and noble people, blessed with abundance and beauty.

In the village of Kaba Kangaba, as in villages throughout Mali, nearly all the women wore gold beads braided into their hair, and great earrings of gold hung from their ears. The rains always came in the rainy season and the granaries were filled with millet, rice, and yams. Like the Fulani and Bella herdsmen from the north, the Malinke villagers raised cattle, and the forest gave them game to hunt. A stone's throw from Kaba Kangaba, the Sankarani River provided fish to eat and fresh water, which the young people carried in water jars and large clay pots from the river to the communal kitchens. And the village was rich in laughter and love, and in music, dance, and crafts as well.

It was a source of great pride to the whole village to be admired by outsiders. If a stranger appeared in their midst, they put on a festive display of music and dance and lavished gifts upon the visitor so that he might later boast of Mali's greatness in his travels. Besides, a number of the elders were members of the Keita clan that, according to tradition, was descended from a wanderer from the east. One never knew if such a stranger might not be the spirit of a returning ancestor.

ankan Musa had just returned from drawing water from the river when a stranger appeared in the small village of Kaba Kangaba. Curiously, no one had seen the man approach. But suddenly there he was. The stranger's robes were the color of a clear blue sky. A turban encircled his head like a white cloud, and his face was veiled so that only the dark slits of his eyes were visible. Kankan wondered if this mysterious visitor might be one of the blue men of the desert. The blue men were said to be fierce nomads who carried long, curved knives, who kept strangely silent in the company of others, and whose skin was the color of indigo.

As the village elders hurried to welcome the stranger, Kankan remembered the dream he had had the night before—a dream in which sorcerers whose faces were hidden had made Kankan's village disappear, leaving him alone in the world.

Water sloshed from the mouth of Kankan's jar and darkened the red earth as he set it down. The stranger turned his eyes toward Kankan and seemed for the moment not to hear the talk of the village elders who had gathered around him. Then he turned back to the elders and said, "I have come far seeking Mali and have found great wealth here. But I must tell your king that great wealth that the world has not seen is worth less to your children's children than a rumor of water to a people dying of thirst."

The elders wondered silently about this stranger who presumed to lecture the king of Mali, but they were much too polite to say anything that might

make a guest feel less than welcome.

"You will have to go to Niani, the capital city, to speak with the *mansa*— that is, the king—of Mali," said Musa Weree with a smile that seemed to mask a secret.

But the stranger showed no interest in Niani. "The king has heard me," he said.

Later, around the flickering light of the evening fire, Kankan and his older brother Abubakari sat with the other young men of their age group among the elders of the village as they sang songs and told stories for the entertainment of their guest. Balla Diallo, the master drummer, played the *balafon* while Kalabi Dauman, the senior griot, recited the epic tale of Sundiata, the crippled child who grew to become a great *simbon*, warrior,

and founder of the empire.

Mamadou Kouyate, the village soothsayer, kept his own counsel, offering only that "It is the wandering dog that finds the old bone." This he said to Kankan, who was sitting beside him, though he obviously intended it for the hearing of all who were present. There was a brief, awkward silence as everyone wondered what he had meant. Then Musa Weree reminded them that just that morning Kouyate had run off a stray dog after catching it sniffing around the bones he used to conjure the ancestors. Everyone laughed except the stranger and the old soothsayer.

The young women of the village brought out milk, sweetmeats, and kola nuts for the visitor. Kola nuts, especially, were considered a luxury among the desert peoples, who prized

them not only for their refreshment, but because the embrace of the "twins"—the two interlocking kernels of the nut—made them a token of friendship.

The stranger loosed his veil, revealing a face so black it was almost blue. He told them his name was Tariq al-Aya and that he was a member of the Tuareg tribe from the north. He told strange tales of the great sea to the west where the world begins and ends and of his travels across the vast desert to the north and east.

It seemed to Kankan that the Tuareg spoke directly to him as he told of a sea of sand whose waving dunes rise and fall as far as the eye can see; where billowing dust hangs on the hot wind, blotting out the horizon during the day; where it can become so cold at night that water turns to diamonds, only to become water again when the sun rises; and where terrible sand storms can eat the flesh off a man's bones and etch the bones to slivers.

He told of the mischievous jinns—genies who cause travelers to see mirages, like green oases full of date palms, flowers, and flowing water where, in reality, there is only more sand. "Jinns can put you to sleep, show you miracles, and even transport you through the air. The desert holds many mysteries," he said. "It is a place where many are lost, but it is also a place where a few truly find themselves.

"And beyond the desert there are worlds where great nations like al-Khemia raise temples to rival the mountains, and wise men go to study and learn. There, too, is Mecca, where all roads converge."

Mecca, Kankan knew, was the sacred city of Islam, the Muslim faith. Like many in Kaba Kangaba, Kankan's family had converted to Islam but, at the same time, they had not given up their traditional religious practices or their belief in the ancestors. And no one from the village had ever been to Mecca.

"Beyond the desert," the stranger added, "few take any notice of the Malinke of Mali."

Kankan bristled at this. He wanted to say that Mali would again be great and to tell of Abubakari's dream of carrying its fame to worlds beyond the western sea. But it was not Kankan's place to speak. He was young yet—only fourteen—and it had been less than a year since he was initiated into the company of the adult men of the village. If he were a *simbon*—a master

hunter who could communicate with the spirits of the forest and bush—he would speak and everyone would listen. But he had not yet hunted his first lion, and for the present he had to sit quietly and listen while others spoke.

Suddenly the night was shattered by loud cries in an unfamiliar tongue rushing in from the darkness. Men on foot and on horses seemed to be everywhere, filling the village with dust and blood and screams. Slave raiders! Kankan and Abubakari ran for their spears. But before they reached their weapons, someone threw a raffia sack over Kankan and he was swallowed up in darkness. Above the noise of the melee he heard his mother and brother calling, "Kankan! Kankan!" But there was nothing he could do. As he was thrown over a

horse and carried away, their voices faded along with the sounds of the chaos that filled the village.

Hours passed. Kankan, angry and ashamed to find himself captured and carried off like a child, saw nothing and heard only the sound of the horses' hooves. He vowed to remain alert and to seize the first opportunity to escape. The horses slowed to a walk, and Kankan listened intently. Perhaps, he thought, the slave raiders would stop to rest and he would have his chance. But they kept moving at this slower pace for many more hours, and eventually Kankan drifted into sleep, exhausted.

s Kankan awakened, he knew that something was different, but at first he could not figure out just what it was. He rubbed the sleep from his eyes and found himself looking at a strange landscape. It was not the millet, rice, or yam fields of Kaba Kangaba. It was not the pastureland where the herdsmen grazed their cattle. It was not the forest. It was nothing! The world seemed to have disappeared.

Then Kankan remembered the raid on his village. He turned around, and a short distance away he saw a camp of four camel-hair tents. Around them he saw horses, camels, and men—blue men, probably Tuareg, in flowing robes, with turbans and veils that left only their eyes visible. The silver handles of their swords glinted in the harsh sunlight from beneath the layered folds of fabric.

Remembering his plan to escape, Kankan rose to his feet but took only a few steps. He was weak. His legs were wobbly, and as he looked around, he realized that there was no place to run—no tree, no rock to hide him—only mile after mile of shifting sand dunes stretching to the horizon in every direction. Heat rising from the sand set the air aquiver. Kankan looked back. The Tuareg nomads were watching him but made no move toward him. It took all of Kankan's strength just to keep standing, so for the present, he sat back down.

One of the blue men gave orders, and a moment later Kankan saw someone approaching who looked familiar. It was Yaya, one of the boys of Kankan's age group who must have

been captured also. Yaya brought him water and something to eat. "Kankan, you have returned," said Yaya. "You were asleep for many days, and the raiders decided only this morning to leave you to die in the desert."

Kankan gradually regained his strength and was not left to die. Instead, he remained a captive of the desert band. Together with the others from his village, he was bound to his captors not by rope but by his need for food and water. The caravan moved in the early morning hours before the sun rose, and rested during the day when the sun was high in the sky. Then, in late afternoon, they would set off again and continue for some time into the night, always moving toward the northeast.

After several days they came to an

oasis where there were date palms and henna trees, houses that were square or rectangular, unlike the round houses of Kankan's village, and a market where traders bartered glass beads, spices, brocade, slaves, and salt for gold.

As they entered the market, Kankan looked back toward the desert from which they had taken refuge and saw another band of blue men on camelback, their voluminous robes billowing, their faces veiled to protect them from the biting winds and blowing sands. As the men drew closer there appeared to be only three of them, then two, then one. Their number had been a mirage, a trick of the desert.

The lone traveler dismounted and approached the captives. He looked over the group and then stopped in front of Kankan, staring at him with hard eyes. Silver talismans to ward off the evil eye encircled his turban and glinted in the afternoon sunlight. He turned and walked away, but returned moments later with one of the slave traders. The lone traveler pointed to Kankan as the men spoke in their strange language. Gold changed hands, and then the slaver grasped Kankan roughly by the arm and pulled him up from where he was sitting on the ground.

Speaking now in Kankan's own language, the lone nomad said, "Come," and turned to walk away. At first Kankan just stood there, but the stranger turned again and repeated, "Come." For now, Kankan thought, there was nothing to do but follow.

The nomad mounted his kneeling camel, and the beast lurched to its feet. Looking down at Kankan and pointing to another animal, the veiled blue black stranger said, "Take that camel and come." Kankan took the reins of the beast and led it out of the oasis and into the open desert, following his uncertain fate. Sadness weighed heavily on his heart. *I am not just a captive, but a slave,* he thought. *And I may never see my village again.*

Late that night they made camp. When Kankan had traveled with the slave raiders, he and the other captives slept in the open. He never saw the inside of the Tuaregs' tents. But this nomad was different. "Come," he said. Cautiously, warily, Kankan entered the camel-hair tent. Inside he found surprising comforts. The ceilings and walls of the tent were hung with silk tapestries, and rich rugs carpeted the floors. Light flickered from three oil wicks, and incense filled the air.

Kankan also spied a curved knife. While the desert wanderer was occupied with laying out food of some sort, he turned his back to Kankan. Kankan picked up the knife and removed it from its sheath. If he moved quickly, he could take the man by surprise. His whole body trembled with readiness, yet something held him back.

With his back still to Kankan, the wanderer poured tea, and said casually, "It is a difficult thing when one is young . . . knowing when to act and when to watch and wait."

Kankan froze where he stood, unable to move a muscle. Had the man seen him pick up the knife? And if so, why had he not turned to defend himself?

"The blood one spills with fearful stabs at phantoms in the dark," said the nomad, "may turn out to be the water from one's own waterskin when the harsh light of day returns to the desert."

The Tuareg's words were a warning, and Kankan knew he was right; even with camels and water, Kankan would never survive alone in this alien world. Kankan slipped the blade back into its sheath and laid it down.

A moment later the nomad turned toward him with an offering of food: pounded millet served with milk and honey in a half calabash, dried meat, tea, and kola nuts. Looking now into Kankan's eyes, the Tuareg counseled, "In the desert, death is always near at hand, as familiar as a frequent guest for whom one has developed deep respect. It is even at times a friend."

He paused and then added, "There is no greater freedom than freedom from the fear of death."

There was something familiar about this man, something that lay just beyond Kankan's recognition.

"Sit and eat," the man commanded. The food looked good and Kankan was very hungry, so for the present, he put aside his vague suspicions and ate.

When Kankan looked up again, he saw the Tuareg had loosed his veil, and to Kankan's amazement, he was the same man who had visited Kaba Kangaba the night the slave raiders came—Tariq al-Aya.

"You!" Kankan jumped to his feet. "My village offered you hospitality."

"And so I offer you the same now," replied Tariq, his voice calm.

"You betrayed us to the slave raiders!" Kankan said.

"I am not one of them," the nomad told him. His words had the ring of truth, but Kankan was reluctant to believe him.

"But you bought me to be your slave," Kankan said accusingly.

"You are your own slave," Tariq replied.

"I was a free member of the Keita clan of the Malinke of Mali," Kankan replied with pride and indignation.

"You don't know who you are," said Tariq.

Kankan felt a familiar sting. He and his brothers, Abubakari and little Sulayman, never knew their father. Whenever the other boys in his village disagreed with Kankan or wanted to tease him, they would say, "You don't even know who you are." Kankan's mother, Koroni, said his father had been a great warrior. More than this she would not say. When Kankan begged to know more, she would whisper in his ear, *"Yere-wolo. To know your father, you must first give birth to yourself."* But Kankan didn't understand how this was possible. Koroni told him *yere-wolo*, giving birth to oneself, involved great magic.

"I bought your freedom with gold," Tariq was saying. "I offered you a camel, but you chose to walk like a slave. Already, you think like a slave. Here in the desert, where death is near, I offer you shelter, food, and water—life—and you think only of slitting my throat when my back is turned. You claim to be a man, but you have not yet mastered the beast within you."

Kankan found himself at a loss for what to do or say.

"Sit," Tariq said. "Sit and eat. The journey is long, but it can only be made one step at a time."

Kankan sat down but did not finish his meal right away. "Where are you going?" he asked.

"Where I am going is of less importance to you than where I have been," Tariq said. "The question is, Where are *you* going?"

"I want to return home to my village," Kankan said.

Tariq shook his head slowly. "You have only just begun your journey. It would not be good to turn back now. You must go on."

"Where?" Kankan asked.

"I cannot tell you where. Only Allah knows. But if you will be guided by him, then I will journey with you awhile. There is much that I can share

with you that may help you to discover *Il-Rah*—the Way, the Path. You have only begun to be tested.

"Take the knife," the nomad commanded. "It is yours. You must handle it with great care; it is tipped with a deadly poison that kills as swiftly as a hand smothers the flame of a lighted wick."

With that, Tariq snuffed out the tiny lights of the oil-wick candles. One, two, three. Suddenly, it was so utterly dark, so still, that Kankan could have been alone in the tent, alone in the desert, alone in the world. For what seemed a long time, he could not even hear the sound of Tariq's breathing. It was as if the nomad had just disappeared. Then he heard him stir and knew from the muffled sounds that he had lain down and was asleep.

Kankan lay down, too. At first he only stared into the darkness, still holding a kola nut tight in his hand, as if clinging to the memories of his life in Kangaba. He heard his mother, Koroni, whispering, *"Yere-wolo."* He thought of Abubakari, venturing into the haunted woods on a dare from the other boys of the village, and talking about how one day he would set sail on the great western sea. And he thought of little Sulayman, who followed Kankan everywhere at home. Soon Kankan, too, was asleep. That night he dreamed of cool water, dipped from a deep well. Kankan had had this dream before, and always when he drank from the well he was transformed into a mighty lion.

ime soon blurred for Kankan Musa. The days ran into weeks and the weeks into months. Above them the sun roared like a lion. In the heat-addled air of the desert, crescent dunes rolled endlessly toward every horizon, interrupted only by barren plateaus of sandstone or volcanic rock and dry riverbeds. Like the dunes, Kankan and Tariq al-Aya wandered from oasis to oasis, sometimes in small caravans with other desert dwellers, sometimes alone. There were long stretches where there was no water at all, when the waterskins were empty. If they had arrived at an oasis to find it had dried up, they surely would have perished.

Tariq al-Aya talked of the ways of the nomadic Tuareg, Wodaabe, and Bedouin. He told of the origins of the Dogon who built their villages on the sheer face of cliffs; of Taghaza, a city built entirely of salt; and another, Baladu, built entirely of copper. He recounted tales of kings and heroes who had journeyed far and, with courage and the help of magical jinns, had subdued fantastic monsters and discovered vast hidden treasures. Sometimes he would sing Tuareg songs about green forests, cool shade, and bubbling streams—things never found in the desert, but which the soul desires. And sometimes they rode in silence—a silence so vast Kankan thought he could hear in it the voice of God.

In almost everything—the stories, the songs, and even the silences—there were valuable lessons. Tariq showed Kankan many things: how to ride camels, how to wrap his turban and veil his face against the desert and the eyes of strangers, where to hide his knife within the folds of his robes, which the blue men call *gandoma*.

"Where is your knife?" Tariq once asked him. Kankan reached to draw the blade from its sheath when suddenly he was blinded by a blur of whirling blue and white cloth.

"Your knife hand is bleeding," Tariq told the stunned Kankan. Kankan looked and saw two thin lines of blood welling up from the back of his right hand. It had happened so quickly that pain did not even know where to look for the wound. Kankan was amazed.

"Teach me to wield the knife with such skill," Kankan demanded.

"One lesson at a time," Tariq responded. "First, never draw your knife until you are ready to use it. The

knife no man ever sees is the deadliest and the best defense. Then," he added, "pray to Allah that you never need it."

Kankan learned that to survive, the desert dweller must constantly be alert to a thousand different signs telling him where he is, where others are, where water and food may be found.

"The circling of a bird, the tracks of a dung beetle, the ripples of a dune, a billowing of tan dust in the distance, shadows, even the desert stillness can tell you things that may preserve your life," Tariq instructed him. "And only after your awareness of such details becomes second nature will the *siyahat*, the rhythm of movement, begin to dissolve the distractions and attachments of the world and allow you to lose yourself in the vast horizon and dazzling sky of the great desert. Then, Kankan Musa, then you may truly find yourself."

When they had traveled together for nearly five years, Kankan and Tariq came to the Agadez oasis at the foot of the mysterious Aïr Mountains. It was much cooler in the mountains, and life took refuge there: birds of prey, hyena, and desert fox. But the mountains were also haunted. Strange rock paintings of fantastic, dreamlike creatures appeared along the path every now and then like warnings that Kankan couldn't understand. He also had the eerie feeling that someone, or some*thing*, was watching them . . . following them.

"Jinns," Tariq said softly, and they continued to ride in silence.

When Tariq and Kankan came upon a cool spring among the fig and wild olive trees, they filled their waterskins and decided to make camp. Just as they were about to unload their camels, Kankan noticed a rock painting in the clearing. This was strange indeed because neither he nor Tariq had seen it when they first arrived. The painting was of a great golden snake that rose up out of a black well and traveled over the waves of the sea toward a rising sun. A mighty lion rode on the snake's head, and many men rode on its back while people of many nations watched in amazement.

Kankan knew he had seen this scene before, in his dreams, but he had never understood its meaning. He and Tariq were so mesmerized by the painting that they didn't notice the jinn rising from the spring like a faint mist. By the time Kankan turned

around, the mist had settled on the bank of the stream, taking the form of a lion. Kankan stood frozen. Slowly, he reached over to warn Tariq, whose back was turned and who seemed still to be looking at the painted rock. But Tariq was not looking at anything. He was sound asleep on his feet. Kankan tried to awaken him, but the nomad would not stir.

"There is no use trying to waken him," the lion said. "He cannot hear you." It was true. Kankan was alone with the beast, alone with his fear, and both eyed him now with the cold stare of a predator stalking its prey. Something he had once heard from the hunters of his village now kept his feet rooted where he stood: *Cats kill with a bite to the back of the neck; their victims are always fleeing.* Kankan knew that he could stand and be the hunter or flee and become the game.

"**W**hat manner of lion are you that you speak to men?" Kankan inquired.

"**I** am Simbon, the mighty hunter who steals upon mighty hunters, a king of beasts and a king of men. What manner of man are you that you heed the speech of beasts?" the lion jinn responded.

The lion was speaking in riddles. Kankan knew that he should take great care with his words now lest he give the wrong response and the lion devour him. He began to feel the panic that Tariq so often warned of creeping up on him. It was the same terror he had felt one night in the Sahel when, gathering twigs for a fire, he met the glowing eyes of a hyena. It was only after the hyena had backed off into the night that Kankan turned to find Tariq, dark and imposing,

behind him. Tariq's words came back to him now: *Neither hyena nor lion nor dragon fish, but fear; fear is the beast that devours a man.* Kankan managed to control this beastly fear, and in so doing found his answer to the lion jinn.

"I am master of the beast," Kankan answered boldly, "and one who hunts the lion."

"In coming face-to-face with the lion, you may discover your own true identity," the lion jinn said. "But be forewarned. If you are not truly master of the beast, the beast will devour you."

The lion then roared a terrible roar and sprang toward Kankan. Kankan's knife flashed from his robes, but in midair the mighty lion dissolved back into a mist that fell gently away.

"The lion wears the trousers of the king," Tariq said. He was awake again and studying the rock painting, unaware that anything unusual had happened or that he had been asleep.

Kankan looked at the rock painting and saw that the lion was indeed wearing the royal trousers of the king of Mali. He would have to think about what that meant later, but for now he thought only of leaving this place.

He mounted his camel. "Come," he said to Tariq. The nomad hesitated, but there was no mistaking the quiet authority in the boy's command. Tariq mounted his camel, and together they continued their trek through the Aïr Mountains. They didn't see the lion again, but they heard its roar echoing through the rock canyons until they reached the desert dunes a few days later.

Once again, a vast sea of sand stretched out before them, reaching to the eastern horizon. "I must visit these worlds beyond the desert you speak of," Kankan told Tariq. Something the lion had said reminded him that there were things he had yet to see and things he had to discover.

"We will go to al-Khemia," Tariq said.

ariq and Kankan journeyed another several months in the desert until one morning as the darkness lifted in the east, Kankan saw three perfect mountains rising in the distance—monuments to a civilization that was older than memory. "This is truly greatness that time cannot erase," Kankan marveled.

"All things yield to time," replied Tariq, "but time yields to these alone."

The Great Pyramids towered above al-Khemia, which some call Egypt. Here the sands of the Sahara meet the waters of the Nile, and the mighty majestic Sphinx, the lion-man, watches the passing of aeons. Here, too, the solitude and silence of the desert suddenly exploded into a world of commotion and confusing sights and sounds.

In the capital city of al-Qahira—which the Arabs call Umm Dunya, "Mother of the World"—men drove camels through the streets where muddy buffalos and donkeys pulled carts laden with trade goods. Traders bartered in the shops of the tailors, bakers, sandal makers, and fish and fruit vendors that lined the maze of alleyways between the sand-colored walls and the brick and stone houses and mosques. Veiled women with babies on their hips carried waterpots on their heads. Little boys shouted from rooftops and slung stones at birds. In the crowded, bustling bazaars, beneath palm trees, merchants sold everything from aromatic spices to carpets to gold and silk. Musicians and dancers, snake charmers, dogs, beggars, and holy men shared the narrow lanes and courtyards. And from the minarets, muezzins wailed, "*Allahu Akbar!*" God is greatest!

Kankan Musa had never seen such intense activity. In al-Qahira he met people from the far corners of the world; many were black, but there were some whose skins were the color of copper or amber, and some who were the color of old ivory. They came from the Mediterranean and beyond, from Greece and Rome, and from farther east of al-Khemia. They were Muslims, Christians, and Jews. Al-Khemia was a land of many prophets, Kankan discovered, and some were shared by Muslims, Christians, and Jews alike.

One such prophet, he learned, was known by a name that is the same as Musa. "In our tongue you would be called Kankan Moses," said one old woman of the Nile. "It means

'unfathered son of a princess.'" Kankan felt the familiar sting—the unfulfilled longing to know his own father. But he listened, and the old woman continued. "It also means 'drawn out of water,'" she said, "as in ancient times the infant Moses was found floating in a basket in the Nile. Moses didn't know his father, but in time he learned the truth about his own identity and later led his people into the desert and onto the Path, the *siyahat* of self-discovery."

"**I**t is the same everywhere," Kankan remarked that night as he and Tariq supped on lamb, dates, and sun-raised bread in a small inn. "Whether man, woman, or nation, we are born into the world and, once born, must set out on a journey to discover just who we are and where we have come from."

A week after Kankan and Tariq arrived in al-Qahira many thousands gathered at the Gate of Conquests—one of sixty gates to the city—to celebrate the return of the annual pilgrim caravan from Mecca, the birthplace of the Prophet Muhammad. "Peace be unto you," the returning pilgrims were greeted. "And unto you be peace," they replied. "May Allah the Beneficent, the Compassionate, the Merciful, bless and preserve you."

The travelers told of the hajj—that is, the pilgrimage—they had made with Bedouins, Persians, Indians, Turks, Arabs, and Syrians, crossing the desert wastes until reaching the gardens and orchards of a paradise they claimed was the navel of the world, where the deep green of the lime, pomegranate, and date trees

provided respite and refreshment, and a bubbling stream of clear, sweet water filled the air with delicious melodies. They talked of miracles—of wells that never ran dry—and told how the beating wings of angels brought a cooling breeze around the sacred shrine of the Kaaba.

But beyond the experience of the hajj, Kankan understood that there was an exchange of ideas and of cultures taking place here, with the peoples of the greatest nations of the world all taking part. And he was dismayed to discover that, as Tariq had said so long ago, few from other lands had heard of the great Sundiata or the empire he had built called Mali.

"**T**hese many tribes have warred against each other, lived together, and traded goods for many generations. They have a common history," Tariq

explained. "Sundiata's conquests are nothing to them. What cause have they to know of Mali?"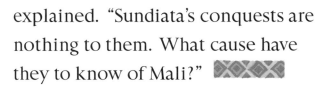

Kankan didn't have the answer to that, but he vowed solemnly that in al-Khemia and in Mecca, where mighty nations meet and their monuments reach to the skies and defy the passage of time, the legends and deeds of Mali, too, would one day be recorded.

But there was much to think about and digest. He had learned a great deal in his six years of wandering with Tariq, and now, after months in the city, the solitude of the desert beckoned to him once again. The desert, where windblown sand quickly covers all tracks, and every traveler must find his own way.

 ankan stood over the last camel where it lay dying in the burning sand. Tariq and Kankan were nearly nine months' travel into the desert. Drought had dried up the wells at the Marzafal oasis, and both their waterskins were now empty. Tariq walked ahead a few paces and was suddenly obscured from Kankan's sight by the dust stirred up by a gust of the hot, dry desert wind. When the dust settled, Tariq was gone. He had vanished as mysteriously as he had appeared in Kaba Kangaba nearly seven years earlier. His tracks in the sand ended only yards from where Kankan stood.

Kankan was alone, utterly alone. As far as he could see, there was nothing but sand and sun. "Look around you," Kankan said to himself, remembering Tariq's words, "as far as you can see . . . freedom." But freedom at that moment felt like pain, like emptiness, like the next gust of wind would dispel his very being as easily as it would the smoke from a quenched candle.

Kankan began walking. *The siyahat, the rhythm of walking, will clear your mind and cleanse your spirit*, he heard Tariq saying. Then he thought he heard other voices in the wind telling him of water, villages, and empires just ahead of him. *Jinns*, Kankan thought. "I'll not be fooled by your tricks," he said quietly, and continued walking west until his strength began to give out. He stopped to rest his legs for a moment, and as he stood staring at the desert before him, the wind began to blow again, moving the desert sands

out like the tides of a vast ocean. Little by little, the winds uncovered the ruins of a walled city that must have been buried there for centuries.

Kankan found himself standing on the roof of one of the buildings. He descended the stone steps that ran down a side wall to an empty courtyard. There he found a gate to this city that might easily have been the capital of a mighty empire; its name, its kings, its people, its noble deeds now lost forever in the sands of time. Kankan was drawn to a door through which he entered a great hall where the air was cool and damp. In the center of this ancient hall stood a well, as big around as the round houses in Kaba Kangaba, filled nearly to the rim with water. Kankan drank the cool, life-saving water from the well and filled his waterskin.

Then, as he peered into the well, the light dancing on the surface of the water gradually formed an image. The image was faint at first, but as it became clearer and stronger, Kankan recognized the great golden snake of his dreams. There it was again, just as he had seen it in the rock painting in the Aïr Mountains, only now it was clear that the snake was not traveling over waves of water but over waving dunes of the desert. The lion in the king's trousers rode the great snake's head with many men behind him. The serpent turned and seemed to move over the desert sands toward Kankan. As it drew closer, the lion's face was transformed. It became human, and strangely familiar. "I am Simbon," said the image in the well, "the mighty hunter who steals upon mighty hunters, a king of beasts and a king of

men. I am Sundiata."

As the image faded from the well, Kankan realized that what he was looking at was his own face reflected in the water. He had not recognized himself at first; months had passed since he'd last seen his own reflection, but it seemed more like ages. There was no mistaking the distinctive features of the noble Keita clan. He was of the Malinke, a child of Mali, and heir to the glory of Sundiata. He had known all along, of course, but the knowing was somehow different now. A deeper knowing. At last, Kankan Musa could say to himself, "I know who I am."

A deep beastly growl caused Kankan to look up from the well. Only a few feet away stood a lion. Was this another jinn who had come to test him or maybe trick him? This lion had

not appeared out of a mist, nor was it talking. This lion looked very real. It watched him with a hunter's eyes. But Kankan was beyond the fear of death.

"I am king of the beast," Kankan said. "You will not devour me."

The lion turned and left the hall. Silently, stealthily, Kankan pursued it through the maze of ancient empty streets. He was a hunter. A *simbon*. Before long, he found himself on the surface of the desert again. The winds blew up a dust storm, and in minutes the ancient city disappeared beneath the sands without a trace. Had it been just a mirage, a trick played on him by the desert jinns? Lion tracks in the sand stretched away toward the west. Kankan felt his waterskin. It was full. He veiled his face against the wind, the sun, and the sand and followed the trail over the dunes. He walked nearly a hundred miles alone in the desert. The wind never covered the lion's tracks, and no matter how much Kankan drank from his waterskin, it remained full.

The landscape changed from sand to grassy savannah as Kankan followed the lion's trail to Timbuktu at the great bend in the Niger River. When he saw the shea butter trees of Mali, he was sure the lion's tracks would lead him home. But then Kankan came to a crossroads, and while he knew Kaba Kangaba was straight ahead, the lion's trail veered to the left, toward Niani, Mali's capital. *Whatever is at the end of this trail—whether lion or jinn or something else*, Kankan thought, *I must pursue it.*

In Niani the trail suddenly ran out. The lion's tracks were lost in the footprints of people. A celebration was taking place. Drummers and dancers filled the streets and everyone was singing songs in praise of the *mansa*, the king of Mali. At first no one seemed to notice Kankan. He was dressed in the robes of the desert nomads of the north. And except for his eyes, his face was hidden by his turban and veil.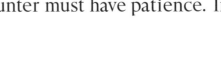

He was surprised to see many there whom he had known from Kaba Kangaba. Though none recognized him now, Musa Weree and the other village elders greeted him warmly and asked if he had come to pay tribute to the new king of Mali.

Kankan's heart overflowed with joy. He wanted to reveal himself and inquire after his mother and brothers, but he waited. Instinctively he knew that the hunt was not over, and above all the hunter must have patience. In the bold manner of the Tuareg who had been his teacher, he said, "A king worthy of tribute is also worthy of trial." The elders of Kaba Kangaba could hardly believe their ears. "For many months," Kankan added, "I have hunted a certain king, and the trail has led me to this place. When I can look into his eyes, I will know whether he is truly king."

"Who is this stranger who comes among us to challenge our king?" the Malinke elders asked themselves.

"I am he who has faced the lion and stood before a mighty sun. I have seen the name of greatness written in the man-made mountains of al-Khemia, and eternity in a vast expanse of open desert. I am he who has seen the fate of Mali written in the ruins of empires now buried and forgotten by time," said Kankan.

The elders sent word of this stranger to the new king. "The *mansa* of Mali says, 'Bring the stranger forward,'" the messenger told them when he returned.

The *mansa* sat on a throne of ebony overarched by large ivory elephant tusks that rose up on each side. He was wearing wide trousers made of a cloth only he was permitted to wear. A young boy at his left held a silk umbrella over him to shade the king from the hot sun. His officers sat around him armed with sabers, lances, quivers, and bows and arrows of gold.

As Kankan approached the throne, he recognized the *mansa*; he was Kankan's own brother Abubakari. And to one side stood their mother, Koroni, still strong as a balanza tree, rooted and unmovable. Sulayman,

now tall and handsome, sat with the council of men. Abubakari waved his fly whisk to signal the drummers and dancers to cease their merrymaking. Kankan, a veiled stranger, stood before Abubakari.

"Welcome, Tuareg. I am told you come to warn the Malinke of times that will turn the happiness you see all around you here to sorrow and regret. Tell me, where should we look for this threat? Mali reigns over the Bilad as-Sudan from the salt mines of Taghaza in the north to as far south as Futa Jallon and the gold-mining districts on the fringe of the rain forests. In the east her dominion extends to where the shea butter trees no longer grow, and in the west, to gold-rich Tekrur and lands reaching all the way to the great sea. One day we will venture beyond even that. So tell me, who

threatens Mali?"

"Mali is indeed great," the stranger acknowledged. "But she has only begun to give birth to herself."

Something in the stranger's voice disturbed Koroni deeply, and when he spoke of Mali giving birth to herself—*yere-wolo* was the phrase he used—she was filled with a sudden painful longing.

"There are worlds away, to the north and east, and perhaps beyond the great sea as well, that have never heard of Mali," he continued. "When your children's children and their descendants for many generations unborn say to those in distant lands, 'I am descended from the Malinke of Mali,' will people ask them, 'Where is Mali?' When the epic tales of great nations are told, will the glories of Mali be remembered, or will some of

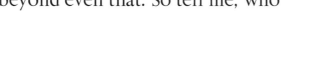

little gold and few victories say that the Malinke went naked in the forests, ate their grains wild, their meat raw, and were fit only to be slaves? Who then will be able to challenge such evil misstatements and say, 'We knew Mali in her glory. Her kings and heroes, her great beauty, and the legend of her might lives on in our memory'?"

Abubakari was not pleased. "Seven years ago, a stranger like yourself entered our midst with warnings," he said. "He was welcomed by the elders who showed him the hospitality of our village. That night, bandits from the north also came and stole my brother and others from us."

"Yes, I remember the night," said the stranger.

"You were among them?" asked the *mansa*.

"Yes," replied the nomad.

"Tell me then, why should I not have you killed?"

"Would you also kill the brother you lost?" the stranger asked.

"You have my brother?" Abubakari asked. "You have brought Kankan Musa? Where is he? Bring him to me that I may see him with my own eyes."

As Abubakari spoke Sulayman stared at the stranger. "Kankan?" he asked.

The stranger loosed his veil and removed his turban. He was no stranger at all. Koroni screamed, and from all who knew him came astonished cries of "Kankan Musa! Kankan Musa! Son of Abu Bekir, son of Sundiata!"

Kankan bowed to his brother, the king, who then lifted him joyfully up into his arms.

Later, Kankan sat up late into the night with Abubakari, Sulayman, and Koroni. Koroni revealed to Kankan that he and his brothers were the grandsons of the great king Sundiata. Their father, Mansa Abu Bekir, had died young, before his sons were old enough to know him, killed by Sakura, who had usurped the throne. Koroni had fled to Kaba Kangaba, where the elders of the Keita clan kept Abu Bekir's family and their secret safe. Then, in the years after Kankan disappeared, Sakura was killed and the people of Mali made Abubakari king. With the Keita clan once more in power, Mali would again be great.

or many years Kankan served as the chief adviser to Abubakari. Where his brother had extended Mali's influence by military might, Kankan helped to consolidate the empire, ensuring the loyalty of its tribute-paying states through diplomacy and trade. Sulayman, a lover of justice, became a law giver and, like his brothers before him, mansa of Mali.

As the challenges facing Mali became fewer and fewer, Abubakari's interest shifted from governing the kingdom to thoughts of realizing a lifelong dream. He commissioned the construction of a massive fleet of ships, turned the empire over to his brother Kankan, and set sail on his own voyage of discovery, in search of lands beyond the western sea. Abubakari never returned.

The seasons came and went, and the bounty of Mali increased manyfold. Kankan Musa, now Mansa Musa, expanded the empire to the north and east, where he gained control of the all-important trading cities of the Sahara, the copper mines of Takedda, and the world-renowned learning centers of Timbuktu and Gao. Mali was said to be four months' travel long and four months' wide, the richest nation in all of Africa.

Like Abubakari, Mansa Musa had not given up the dream of carrying the name of Mali abroad. The time had come, and Mansa Musa made plans to cross the desert once again, this time to make the pilgrimage to Mecca.

For the journey, Mansa Musa assembled a caravan of a size that had never been seen before. The train of sixty thousand courtiers and servants included the king's personal retinue of twelve thousand attendants, all dressed in brocade and Persian silk. Five hundred others each carried a staff of gold weighing six pounds. Behind Mansa Musa walked eighty gold-laden camels, each carrying three hundred pounds of gold bars and gold dust. And riding at the head of this golden caravan that snaked its way over the sands was Mansa Musa himself, the Lion of Mali.

Word of this dazzling spectacle spread far and wide, and the name of Mali echoed throughout the great empires of the world. Mansa Musa was very generous, and he distributed his wealth freely as he traveled, making gifts of gold to foreign rulers and courtiers and the poor. Many who might never have made the pilgrimage were invited to join his caravan. Wherever he went, he built mosques, palaces, and universities. And when he returned to Mali two years later, he brought back scholars, jurists, architects, and advisers. At last the whole world knew of Mali and of the great Mansa Musa.

AUTHOR'S NOTE

How much of *Mansa Musa: The Lion of Mali* is fiction and how much is fact?

The history of the great empire of Mali, including the information provided in the epilogue of this tale, is well documented. There are many scholarly sources that tell of Mansa Musa's golden caravan crossing the Sahara. The wealth and splendor he displayed on this journey were the talk of the Middle East and Europe for many years. One medieval map called him the king of all of Africa. Another European map from the fourteenth century, found in the *Atlas Catalan*, described Mansa Musa's Mali this way: "So abundant is the gold which is found in his country that he is the richest and most noble king in all the land." During Mansa Musa's reign, the Malian Empire was larger than Egypt and its wealth far greater.

The story that Abubakari commissioned a fleet of ships to sail across the Atlantic Ocean in the fourteenth century has also been documented by a number of historians. And some of them point to traditional African roundhouses, huge stone carvings of heads with African facial features, and black-skinned people in Mexico and Brazil as evidence that Abubakari and his men made it all the way to the New World before Columbus.

The background for our story—the places described and the customs of the Malinke (who are also known as the Mandinka) and the Tuareg—is all historically accurate. For example, there actually was a salt city, Taghaza. Its houses and mosques were built of blocks of salt with roofs made of camel skins.

Some historians claim that Mansa Musa was the grandson of the great Sundiata, who was the founder of Mali, and others believe he was Sundiata's grandnephew. Most agree that he became the *mansa* of Mali in 1312 and died in 1337. He probably had a typical upbringing for his village and his time, but hardly anything is known for certain about the particulars of his childhood, and this is the part of the story that I have created.

Finally, the village of Kaba Kangaba still stands in Mali, and the noble Keita clan remains highly respected. One of Mansa Musa's descendants, Salif Keita, is today an internationally renowned Malian singer and musician.

You can read more about Mansa Musa, Mali, and the history of West Africa's great empires in the following books. You can see a picture of the *Atlas Catalan's* European map in *The World in 1492* or at http://www. humanities.ccny.cuny.edu/history/reader/mansamap. htm.

Atmore, Anthony, and Gillian Stacey. *Black Kingdoms, Black Peoples: The West African Heritage*. Photographs by Werner Forman. New York: G. P. Putnam's Sons, 1979.

Chu, Daniel, and Elliott Skinner. *A Glorious Age in Africa: The Story of Three Great African Empires*. Trenton, NJ: Africa World Press, 1992.

Davidson, Basil, and the Editors of Time-Life Books. *African Kingdoms*. New York: Time, 1966.

Fritz, Jean, Katherine Paterson, Patricia and Frederick McKissack et al. *The World in 1492*. New York: Henry Holt and Company, 1992.

Murray, Jocelyn, ed. *Cultural Atlas of Africa*. New York: Facts on File, 1981.